KING ARTHUR

A DK PUBLISHING BOOK
www.dk.com

A RETELLING BASED ON TRADITIONAL SOURCES

Art Editor Lisa Lanzarini
Senior Editor Alastair Dougall
Editor Rebecca Smith
US Editor Kristin Ward
Production Katy Holmes
Managing Art Editor Jacquie Gulliver
Picture Research Louise Thomas
DTP Designer Kim Browne

For Jennifer with lots of love – RK　*For Theo – TH*

Reprinted 1999

4 6 8 10 9 7 5 3

Published in the United States by DK Publishing, Inc.
95 Madison Avenue New York, NY 10016

Library of Congress Cataloging-in-Publication Data
Kerven, Rosalind.
King Arthur / retold by Rosalind Kerven: illustrated by Tudor Humphries. — 1st American ed.
p. cm. — (An eyewitness classic)
Summary: A retelling of the boy fated to be the "Once and Future King," covering his glorious reign and his tragic, yet triumphant, passing. Illustrated notes throughout the text explain the historical background of the story.
ISBN 0-7894-2887-3
1. Arthurian romances — Adaptations. [1. Arthur, King — Legends. 2. Knights and knighthood — Folklore. 3. Folklore — England.]
I. Humphries, Tudor, ill. II. Malory, Thomas, Sir, 15th cent. Morte d'Arthur. III. Title. IV. Series.
PZ8.1.K45Kaar 1998
398.2 ' 0942 ' 02 — dc21   97-32301
                                                    CIP
                                                    AC
Color reproduction by Bright Arts in Hong Kong
Printed by Graphicom in Italy

EYEWITNESS CLASSICS

KING ARTHUR

ROSALIND KERVEN

Illustrated by
TUDOR HUMPHRIES

DK

DK PUBLISHING, INC.

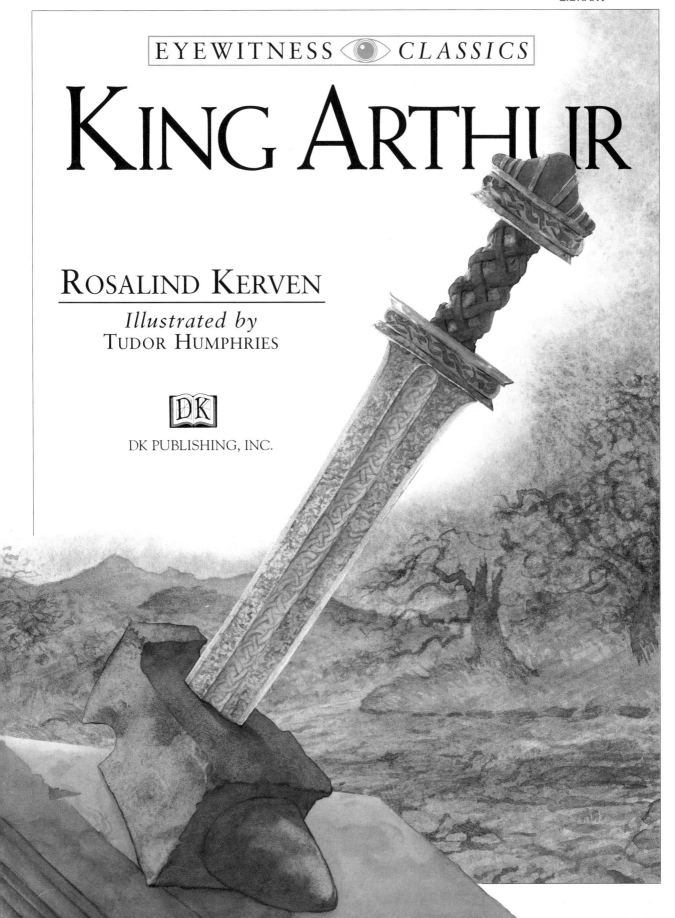

Contents

King Arthur   *Guinevere*   *Merlin*   *Nimue,*
the Lady of the Lake   *Morgan le Fay*

Sir Lancelot

Nascien

Sir Galahad

Sir Bors

Sir Mordred

INTRODUCTION

The story of Arthur, the heroic king who created the most glorious realm in Europe, has its source in the anarchy that arose when the Romans left Britain, early in the 5th century AD. The Romans had brought order; they had built towns linked by well-made roads; they had brought the Christian faith. All these achievements began to decay when they left. The native Celtic people split into warring kingdoms and were beset by invaders. Out of this chaos, perhaps as an expression of people's longing for a better world, the legendary figure of Arthur was born.

Tales of his marvelous exploits were sung by Celtic bards and told around the fireside for hundreds of years before being written down in the Middle Ages. Ever since, Arthur's legend has grown, like a great river fed by many streams.

With color photographs and paintings to bring to life its historical background, this Eyewitness Classic retelling evokes the legend's authentic, Celtic atmosphere of magic and mystery. Wonders appear, swords clash, plots are hatched, brave words are spoken, and even braver deeds performed, as we return to the Castle of Camelot in the golden age of King Arthur, Queen Guinevere, Sir Lancelot, and the Knights of the Round Table.

Bamburgh Castle, Northumberland, legendary home of Sir Lancelot

Ancient woods

The story begins late in the 5th century, after the Romans had left Britain. Most of the country was a lawless wilderness of forests, marshes, and moorlands, where armed men roamed at will.

The last Druid?

The all-knowing figure of Merlin may have been inspired by native Celtic priests called Druids. The Druids were very powerful in Britain until the 1st century AD, when they were crushed by the invading Romans.

Chapter one

THE SWORD IN THE STONE

THE OLD KING WAS DEAD. The throne was empty, the crown unclaimed, and fear crept like a glowering storm-shadow across the land. Without a king, there were no laws. Without laws, the land was soon overrun by ruthless invaders and local warlords. Gangs of coarse men forced their way through the villages, stealing cattle and treasure, breaking down doors, snatching away children. Without a new king – a good, strong king – there was no hope, but only the promise of more darkness, more fear.

Out of this darkness, through the secret paths of the Great Forest, a strange figure came walking, the figure of a wizard. His name was Merlin.

This Merlin, he was as old as oak roots; he could catch the wind and weave it into poems; his black eyes could read the future and his spells could change it. He saw the future now as he walked toward it, a time of sunshine, gold, and glory, the glory of a great new king. Merlin knew the name of that king and where he was hidden, for his own wizardry had overseen the boy's birth and hidden him away from evil and danger. Now that boy's time had come.

Merlin stepped out of the forest. He was a tall, gaunt, long-bearded figure, muttering in strange tongues, wrapped in a gray cloak, bent against the driving rain. Leaving the trees behind him, he strode along the open road that led to the city of London.

Merlin strode along the open road that led to the city of London.

By the time
Merlin reached
the city walls, the
road was swarming
with tough, armed men
brandishing spears and swords.
They were all warlords, come to
fight to the death for the crown of Britain.
It had been agreed that whoever could
slaughter most of his rivals should become king.

Dusk fell. Like a shadow, the old wizard slipped
through the jostling warriors. The city gates opened at
his whisper and he passed through them into the winding
streets of London.

There was no-one about. Every door was bolted against the
coming battle. Not a dog barked, not a child cried out; only the
hoot of an early owl disturbed the nervous stillness. Merlin hurried on,
towards the yard of London's Great Church.

He sat down there, and waited.

The night passed uneasily, lit by neither moon nor stars. At last, morning came.
A line of monks led by a bishop walked into the churchyard, on their way to prayer.
Merlin rose and bowed to them; then he pointed across the yard.

"My brothers," he called, "Over there – look!" They all turned.

On the cropped grass in front of the church, something strange and marvellous had
appeared. It was a huge slab of marble stone, with an iron anvil on its top; and thrust through
both anvil and stone was a sword.

The sword was heavy, gleaming, beautiful; and upon the marble stone was carved in flowing
golden letters:

WHERE IS THE MAN
WHO CAN PULL THE SWORD FROM THE STONE?
HE IS THE RIGHTFUL KING OF BRITAIN

As the monks stared at it, Merlin bowed again. "Peace, my brothers," he said.
"Send the watchmen to open the gates. Let the warlords come in and show them
the stone. Tell them this: the battle is over before it has even begun. Let the new
king claim his sword!"

On the cropped grass in front of
the church, something strange and
marvellous had appeared.

The grip was
covered with
wood, bone, or
leather

Weapon of power
At this time, swords
were made of iron
with decorated
hilts. Only high-
ranking warriors
could afford them. In
this episode, the sword
symbolizes masculine
power. The image of a
sword embedded in an
anvil is a clear invitation
for one man to take
control – but who?

Long, wide,
double-edged
blade

Celtic
cross

**In
ruins**
London's
Great Church
had been
damaged by
looters. It was
built where
Westmister
Abbey now
stands.

Newly forged
An anvil is an iron block
on which metal weapons
were shaped. The sword in
this anvil holds a brand-
new promise of power.

Tintagel Castle
One tradition claims that Arthur was born at Tintagel, Cornwall. His father, King Uther Pendragon, fell in love with Igraine, wife of Gorlois, Duke of Tintagel. Merlin transformed Uther into an exact likeness of Gorlois. Thus disguised, Uther visited Igraine and made love to her, and Arthur was born.

Merlin and the baby
Merlin prophesied a glorious future for Arthur, but, fearing for his safety, he insisted that the newborn baby be handed over to his care. He secretly took him to be fostered by a knight called Ector, who brought up Arthur to be a cultured warrior-nobleman, alongside Ector's own son, Kay.

The city gates were flung open, north, south, east, and west. The rival warlords and their gangs came stamping in.

They marched to the Great Church. There they saw the marble stone, the anvil, and the sword; they read the gold inscription; they noticed the old wizard waiting for them nearby. There was power here, stronger than their own brute force: it made them stop and catch their breath.

Merlin spoke: "My friends, let each man take his fair turn to pull the sword from the stone. The lords shall try first. If none succeeds, the common soldiers shall all attempt it. Give every man a chance – even the youngest and most humble. I urge you to be patient! For God knows that only one man in Britain is destined to pull this sword from the stone, and before the end of today, you shall all know who he is."

So the contest began.

The fiercest of the warlords gripped the sword, tensed his muscles, strained and heaved. But the shining blade remained stuck fast. The other chieftains who came after him did no better. They all turned away, cursing in disgust; and then the soldiers crowded around, pushing forward for their turns, on and on through the long day. But they all failed, too.

As the sun began to set, a youth stepped forward. He was tall and broad. He did not swagger like the others, nor did he hesitate, but strode to the marble with an easy grace.

The youth gripped the sword. Lightly, he pulled on it. And at once – it came clean out from the stone.

A gasp of outrage ran through the crowd.

Merlin whirled around to face them. "You have seen him do it," he cried. "He is the one!" He turned to the youth. "Your name, sir?"

"I am Arthur."

"Arthur," echoed Merlin, "I know this Arthur." His voice rang out eerily into the tense air. "He is no ordinary youth, but the long-lost love child of our old king, good King Uther Pendragon. This boy, he was conceived in mist, born in a storm, smuggled away to be raised in secrecy. Now his time has come. Put your faith in him! For I swear by all the gold in Britain, this Arthur will lead you into such glory ..."

But Merlin's words were drowned in uproar.

The youth gripped the sword. Lightly, he pulled on it. And at once – it came clean out from the stone.

The watching warriors, maddened by their own frustration and failure, surged forward, swords and axes gleaming. For every man there was seized with a sudden desire to kill the wizard and the youth.

Arthur's gleaming blade flashed in the twilight.

Arthur raised the Sword high above his head. The gleaming blade flashed in the twilight. The first warrior came at him.

Arthur moved like wildfire. Skillfully, he turned each sword-blow back at his attacker until he had him sprawling on the ground, begging for mercy. Without a pause, another warrior was on him, then more of them, until Arthur was fighting at once in all directions. But he seemed scarcely scratched by their blows, and he fended off each one of them with ease.

Before long his challengers were falling back, and their anger had turned to amazement. Arthur leaned on the Sword.

"Listen!" he shouted. "You saw just now that I could easily have killed every man who attacked me – but I chose to let you all live. I'll tell you why. I believe it's a waste of time and strength – a madness – for us to fight each other. We're destroying the whole kingdom – and giving our enemies a chance to seize it!"

Silence answered him. He went on:

"I've just proved that no one can beat me! If you were to fight with me, instead of against me – if you were to accept me as your king – then we could drive our enemies out of Britain once and for all!

"Then I will bring you peace and give you what you long for most, my lords. Power! Wealth! Yes! You shall each have your own castle, your own land, your own people, within my kingdom. And I shall give you gold! I swear that each lord who takes an oath of friendship shall have a share of treasure from the royal coffers."

Arthur's hands, resting on the Sword, were trembling now. His gaze swept steadily across the suspicious throng.

Still no one spoke.

The last light faded from the day. Torches were lit, and the sweet notes of evensong drifted from the church.

At last, murmurs began to spread through the crowd:

"Strong words, those ..."

"Wiser than his years ..."

"No harm to give him a chance ..."

In the torchlight, Merlin put a hand on Arthur's shoulder. "Arthur will be crowned here at Easter," he said. The crowd watched, mesmerized, as he turned and led the youth away..

Foreign invaders
The main enemies of Britain were the Saxons, Angles, and Jutes from northern Germany and Scandinavia, who were occupying what is now eastern England. At the same time the Franks were invading the southeastern coast and the Picts were raiding the north. Some Britons decided to escape by ship to Brittany in France.

Anglo-Saxon helmet

The Anglo-Saxon threat
At first British chiefs welcomed the Anglo-Saxons as allies in wars against each other. Anglo-Saxon warriors were paid with land in eastern Britain. As their numbers and their power grew, the Anglo-Saxons turned on their former allies, seizing their land.

MAGIC AND MYSTERY

The legends of Arthur evoke a world when magic was respected
and feared – a time when people believed in sorcery, shape-
changing, omens, and treasures with miraculous powers. The roots of
this magic lie deep in Celtic traditions, for the Celts believed
supernatural forces were all around them – in the air, in the sun,
moon, and stars, in the seas, mountains, rivers, trees, and stones.
Only those specially gifted by the gods knew how to communicate
with these forces to create magic. Arthur's story is dominated by
two characters who use magic to decide his fate, and that of the
kingdom – the wizard Merlin and the witch Morgan le Fay.

*A wizard's
staff – sign
of power and
magic tool*

The magnificent ruins of Stonehenge, Wiltshire

Standing stones

According to legend,
Merlin's magical powers arranged
the immense stone circle at
Stonehenge. This ancient temple
may have played a vital role in
Druidic rituals connected with
fertility and the passing of the
seasons. Like a massive sundial,
the stones are positioned so that
sunrise on midsummer day, June 21,
appears behind a central stone called
the Heel stone.

*In the tales of Arthur, woods
and forests are dark, enchanted
places where knights face
supernatural dangers.*

The twisted oaks of Wistman's Wood, Dartmoor

*Merlin's magic
manipulates the
forces of nature.*

Morgan le Fay

Morgan le Fay is a witch, rumored to be of fairy descent ("Fay" means fairy). She learned much of her magic from Merlin but, unlike him, she prefers to use it for her own evil purposes. Her chief goal is to bring down Arthur, her own half-brother, yet some legends claim that she has a good side and has great gifts as a healer. She is adept at creating poisons and sleeping potions from herbs. She is able to fly and can transform herself, and others, into animals and rocks.

Morgan le Fay

One of Morgan's favorite guises

Thunder and lightning were powerful evidence of the gods' supreme power.

Dozmary Pool in Devon is a famous haunt of lake spirits such as the Lady of the Lake.

LAKE SPIRITS

Lakes and pools were haunted by powerful, nymphlike spirits, such as the Lady of the Lake. People gained the favor of these spirits by throwing precious objects into the waters of lakes such as Dozmary Pool on Bodmin Moor (above left), which, according to legend, may be the pool where Sir Bedivere threw Arthur's sword, Excalibur.

Lake spirits were traditionally beautiful and mysterious.

Excalibur

Forged by fairy smiths on the isle of Avalon, Arthur's sword Excalibur is a weapon of magical power, a precious gift from the Lady of the Lake. No enemy can withstand its blade.

The Celts believed that spirits dwelled in rocks and stones. Certain stones might detect a lie, or reveal a rightful ruler by shouting with joy.

Arthur accepts Excalibur from the Lady of the Lake in the 1981 film Excalibur.

King Arthur's castle
Camelot was the legendary home of Arthur. As the legend grew, Camelot came to represent a mystical, imaginary, golden place – a symbol of harmony and a center of virtue. The Camelot shown above, from the movie First Knight (1995), romantically portrays Arthur's headquarters as a magnificent fairy-tale castle.

Chapter two

THE GIFT OF EXCALIBUR

NEWS SPREAD QUICKLY of the coming of a new king who promised to rid the land of invaders and bring an end to pointless wars. Those lords who refused to accept the new king were soon defeated and, by Easter, the whole of Britain was won over to Arthur's side. The invaders realized that they could never overcome such a united country, and withdrew. At long last Britain was blessed by prosperity and peace.

Then every man and woman with strength to ride to London came to see Arthur crowned. After the ceremony he invited the nobles to a feast, and there he handed out many fine gifts of land and treasure. Then he rode away with Merlin, to make his court at Camelot.

Time passed. One day Arthur said to Merlin, "Good wizard, you know I left the Sword in the Stone by the Great Church, for that is its rightful place. But I need a weapon of my own – one fit for a king."

"Saddle your horse and follow me," said Merlin.

They rode out of Camelot, deep into the Great Forest. In time they came to a vast, shimmering lake.

"Wait," said Merlin, "and watch."

A wind blew up. The still waters rippled. From their midst, there appeared a graceful arm, draped in pure white silk; and grasped in the hand was a sword. As Arthur stared at it, a woman came walking toward him, skimming lightly over the surface of the water. She plucked the sword from the hand as she passed, slid it into an exquisitely worked scabbard, and offered the hilt to Arthur.

"I am Nimue, Lady of the Lake," she said, "and this sword is called Excalibur. It was forged by fairy smiths in Avalon and I have kept it safe through countless seasons, especially for you."

Arthur took it and bowed. "I am greatly honored," he said.

The lady laughed. "Tell me, do you like it?"

"It is a treasure," said Arthur.

"Ah," she said. "It is true that Excalibur will win you many battles; but remember this, Arthur: its *scabbard* is worth more to you than a thousand swords. For while you wear it at your side, you will never die of any wound; but if this scabbard should ever be lost – oh, Arthur, then beware!"

"I will remember your words and guard it well," said Arthur.

"Then, farewell good King, farewell old Wizard," said Nimue.

And she faded away like the mist.

Nimue the nymph
Nimue is similar to nature spirits called nymphs who often appear in Greek and Roman myths. Legend says that Nimue's father was a worshipper of Artemis, the Greek goddess of hunting, woods, and lakes and that Nimue was protected by the goddess. In Arthur's story, Nimue is a magical figure second only to Merlin in power.

A woman came walking toward Arthur, skimming lightly over the water.

Arthur was struck by Guinevere's copper-haired beauty.

The young king grew into a fine man. His skill as a warrior was already legendary. Now other stories spread about him: how he could hunt the stag for seven whole days without ever tiring; how when a feast was held at Camelot, he would lead the dancing past midnight into dawn; how he could calm any quarrel with a few light words, and soothe any sadness with his smile.

Britain was basking in peace. Arthur and Merlin rode up and down the byways of the land, sealing old friendships and making new ones.

One evening they were riding through the rolling countryside of Cameliard. Arriving at the castle of King Leodegrance, they asked for lodging for the night.

They were welcomed into the hall by Guinevere, the king's only daughter. Arthur was struck by her copper-haired beauty and the way her eyes were alive with dancing sea-lights. She was not awed to meet the famous Arthur. With her own hands she offered him a drinking-horn brimming with fine wine, and asked him what news he brought from Camelot.

Arthur surprised himself by how much he had to tell her. Guinevere listened to him intently. The servants brought in dishes of meat, fruit, and honey, and threw logs onto the fire. Then it was Guinevere's turn to talk, and Arthur's to listen.

At the evening's end, Guinevere's father came home.

Arthur jumped to his feet and bowed deeply.

"Sir," he said, "I beg you to grant me a boon. Let me marry your daughter! I would like to make her my queen."

King Leodegrance considered his reply. "Young man," he said. "Many fathers would give their lives for such an honor. You have my warmest blessing."

Arthur nodded and turned to Guinevere. "My lady, will you accept me as your husband?"

Guinevere smiled. "I will," she said.

And so the wedding was arranged, and there was great joy. But next morning, when Arthur and Merlin were riding back to Camelot, the old wizard shook his head and sighed.

"You may think that love is everything, Arthur," he said, "but I fear you will regret your wedding day. For I dreamed last night that Guinevere will bring about your doom."

But Arthur only laughed at the wizard's mournful words.

Women of power
In some Celtic societies, noblewomen participated considerably in politics. One warrior-queen, Boudicca (pictured above), even led a revolt against Roman rule in Britain in AD 60. As queen, Guinevere would have expected to play an important part in governing the kingdom.

Celtic queen
Celtic women prided themselves on their beauty, particularly their elaborately styled hair. Painters have often celebrated them – this portrait of Queen Guinevere is by Victorian artist William Morris.

Arthur made his court at Camelot.

Chapter three

THE KNIGHTS OF THE ROUND TABLE

A royal wedding
Arthur's and Guinevere's marriage – sumptuously portrayed here in the 1981 movie Excalibur *– heralds the dawning of the fellowship of the Round Table.*

Among equals
The Round Table is a lasting symbol of equality. A "round-table discussion" now means a meeting where everyone is on equal terms. This medieval table is at Winchester Castle, England.

SHORTLY BEFORE the wedding, Leodegrance escorted Guinevere to Camelot. He also brought his wedding gift: a massive, round, oak-wood table. Arthur watched as it was carried into the castle's great hall.

Leodegrance said: "Each place at this table is meant to seat a knight. If you meet regularly with your followers, Arthur, and talk with them openly, they are less likely to grow resentful or brood on dangerous secrets."

"But a king's place is at the head of the table – and there is no such seat within a circle," said Arthur.

Guinevere took his hand. "When you sit at this table, my lord, you should let all men have an equal voice."

"Even so," he said, "there may be quarrels over who should sit where."

Merlin stepped forward. "Let me put an end to such evil before it can begin." He held his gnarled hands out toward the Round Table. Sparks crackled from his long, clawlike nails and the Table shimmered. Now names were carved in the polished wood, one by every seat.

"These are the names of all the Knights of the Round Table," said Merlin. "Some have already arrived in Camelot; many more are on their way."

"I will welcome them with all my heart," said Arthur.

But a moment later, he pointed at one of the places at the Table. "There is no name here, only the words 'Siege Perilous.'"

"Ah," said Merlin softly, "that is an enchanted place – the 'Seat of Danger.' It is for one man only: if any other should sit there he will be burned away to ashes!"

He led Arthur to the door, and the king saw many knights riding over the green hills toward Camelot. They came from every corner of the kingdom, and even from beyond its shores, and each was fine and noble as only a knight can be.

The knights came from every corner of the kingdom.

The white hart

In Christian art, a white hart symbolized purity. A white hart (a male red deer) being chased by hounds – purity pursued by evil – is a call to arms the knights should not have ignored.

Thrills of the chase

Dogs similar to the modern-day Irish wolfhound were used to hunt deer and wild boar in the forests of the kingdom. The sport (pictured below) had been popular with nobles and warriors since pre-Roman times, and legend claims that Arthur was a great hunter.

Arthur and Guinevere were married in a little church that stood by Camelot. Afterward there was a grand celebration at the castle. Halfway through the wedding feast, the castle door burst open, and a white deer-hart came bounding in, pursued by sixty yelping hounds. Next, a lady ran in, shrieking that the hart was her pet and must not be killed; and she in turn was chased by a villainous-looking fellow – who forced her onto his horse and carried her, screaming, away.

There was a shocked hush. It was broken by Queen Guinevere's clear, sweet voice: "That lady is in great distress." She gazed around the hall. "Who will go to save her?"

Not one knight answered.

A white deer-hart came bounding in, pursued by sixty yelping hounds.

"Shame on you!" she cried. "If Arthur were asking for volunteers to go to war, you would all be clamoring to fight. Isn't a lady's terror more deserving than some squabble over a piece of gold or land?"

Every man shifted uncomfortably.

"You, you, and you!" Guinevere pointed a slim finger at Sir Gawain, Sir Tor, and Sir Pellinor. "Follow that poor lady and do not return until you have rescued her!"

The three bowed to the queen and went out. Then Guinevere took Arthur's hand and led him away to talk privately outside.

Hours passed. Lamps were lit and the dancing began. Arthur and Guinevere came back into the hall, but did not join in the cheer.

At last, the three knights returned, bringing with them the lady of the white hart. The queen welcomed the lady and thanked the knights. Then the king called for silence.

"Listen, men of the Round Table!" said he. "From today, you must serve the queen as well as me. Together we command you to strive for justice – not for brute power! Never shall you refuse help to any woman; you must protect the weak and innocent; you must always be merciful and kind!"

One after another, the knights stepped forward and swore upon the Bible to obey. But there were some who glowered at the queen, and muttered that a woman of such spirit deserved a bitter downfall.

Swearing on the Bible
The Christian knights swore the Round Table oath by placing their right hands on a Bible. Their promise, to protect women and uphold justice, is the basis for a code of knightly conduct called chivalry.

KNIGHTS OF KING ARTHUR

The best knights of Britain and Europe took their places at the Round Table of King Arthur. Soon the king and his court became famous for their bravery, generosity, and high moral code. Each knight swore, on pain of death, to be loyal to the king; to be merciful; to defend women; and never to fight in any wrongful cause. As the legends grew, the characters of those knights that played crucial parts in the rise and fall of Arthur's court were established. Featured here are some of the most important, and some of their most marvelous adventures.

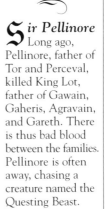

This French medieval illustration of the Round Table shows only 12 knights, but accounts claim there were as many as 1,600.

Sir Bedivere
One of the first knights to join the Round Table, Bedivere is largely responsible for the many tournaments and feasts held at Camelot. He remains with Arthur until the end, when his loyalty is tested as never before.

Sir Bors
The son of the King of Gaul (France) and Sir Lancelot's cousin, Bors is one of the most virtuous knights and a close comrade of Galahad and Perceval – younger knights who place spiritual matters above worldly pleasure.

Sir Galahad
Youthful Sir Galahad is the Round Table's most saintly knight. In battle he wears red armor to symbolize the blood of Jesus Christ, and carries a white shield with a red cross. For years a special seat at the Round Table awaited him.

Sir Gawain
Arthur's nephew, and the eldest son of King Lot of Orkney, Gawain is second only to Lancelot as a fighter, and surpasses him in loyalty. However Gawain can be fiercely proud, quick to take offense and seek revenge.

Sir Gareth
A close friend of Lancelot, Gareth is considerate and kind, unlike his proud elder brothers Gawain and Gaheris, and his cruel, scheming other brother, Agravain.

Sir Kay
Arthur's foster-brother, Kay is Arthur's steward, supervising the running of Camelot. He is bad-tempered and a poor fighter, but very loyal.

Sir Mordred
Some say that Mordred is Arthur's nephew by his sister Anna. On the day of Mordred's birth, wizard Merlin makes a dire prophecy: that Mordred will seize Arthur's crown.

Sir Pellinore
Long ago, Pellinore, father of Tor and Perceval, killed King Lot, father of Gawain, Gaheris, Agravain, and Gareth. There is thus bad blood between the families. Pellinore is often away, chasing a creature named the Questing Beast.

Sir Perceval
Perceval is one of the Round Table's greatest warriors – third behind Lancelot and Galahad. He has an aura of almost saint-like innocence and humility.

Sir Tristan
Tristan arrives at Camelot pining for the love of his uncle's wife Iseult. He does not stay at Camelot long, but proves himself a mighty warrior – even matching Lancelot, who later becomes a close friend.

Victorian actor Forbes Robertson as Lancelot, the Queen's Champion

Gawain (Murray Head) bares his neck to the axe of the Green Knight (Nigel Green) in the 1973 film.

The Queen's Champion
On the day Arthur is to make him a knight, handsome young Lancelot discovers he has forgotten his sword. Queen Guinevere finds him one and Lancelot swears never to serve any other woman. He soon becomes the Queen's Champion and the Round Table's greatest and most fearless warrior. Lancelot's seat at the Round Table is on the right of his son Galahad's.

Gawain and the Green Knight

A giant knight dressed in green challenges the Round Table: any man may strike a blow against him, if he may strike a blow in return in a year and a day. Gawain takes the giant's ax and cuts off his head. The giant picks up his head and rides off.

A year passes and Gawain sets out on his quest. A knight's wife tries to make him fall in love with her. He resists, but accepts a belt, which she says will protect him. Gawain meets the Green Knight and bares his neck. Twice the giant pretends to strike. The third time, he nicks Gawain with his ax. Gawain has proved his worth – his only fault accepting the belt from a married lady.

Celtic ax

Tristan and Iseult

Tristan, King Mark of Cornwall's nephew, goes to fetch the king's young bride, Iseult, from Ireland. On board ship, he and Iseult accidentally drink a love potion. Mark and Iseult are wed, but she and Tristan meet in secret. Mark finds out and banishes Tristan. He travels to France, where he marries another lady called Iseult; but he never forgets his former love. Wounded in battle, he begs his wife to send for Iseult – only her skill can heal him. It is arranged that if Iseult is coming, her ship will fly white sails, if not, black sails. Tristan's jealous wife sees a ship with white sails, but tells Tristan they are black. Believing Iseult no longer loves him, he dies. Iseult finds Tristan's body and dies of a broken heart.

Tristan and Iseult drink a love potion, painted in 1912 by John McKirdy.

The Knight of the Kitchen

Gareth arrives at Camelot disguised as a servant and is given a job in the kitchens. One day a lady named Lynet comes seeking a champion to rescue her sister, Lyonors. Gareth begs Arthur to let him go on the quest. Lynet says Gareth smells of the kitchens, but he proves his skill and bravery, overcoming the Black, Green, and Red Knights. Finally he vanquishes Lyonors's captor, the cruel Red Knight of the Red Lawns, and marries the beautiful Lady Lyonors.

Gareth and Lynet – a 1902 illustration by H. J. Ford.

Lancelot's sinister discovery

One of Lancelot's strangest adventures begins when a weeping maiden tells him that her lover has been killed by the knights of the castle of Dolorous Garde. Lancelot kills the knights thanks to a shield sent him by the Lady of the Lake which gives him the strength of three men. After freeing many prisoners, he is taken to a graveyard where lies an iron slab that only he who conquers the castle may lift. Lancelot lifts the slab and reads: "Here shall lie Lancelot of the Lake" – it is his own tomb.

Lancelot in battle, by N. C. Wyeth (1927).

Lancelot lifts the cover of his own grave – a 14th-century illustration.

*Merlin made a spell
to bind Nimue
to his side.*

Chapter four

EVIL ENCHANTMENTS

NEVER HAD THERE been such a majestic court as Camelot. The whole world sang the praises of its brave and generous king. As the years went by, Arthur grew mellow and warm as old wine. His store of wisdom grew and he no longer turned to Merlin for advice. The ancient wizard's pride was badly hurt by this change. He grew jealous to see how Arthur now only confided in Guinevere. "What!" he thought. "Here am I, nearly seven centuries old, and I have never yet tasted the fruits of love!"

He began to search through all the shadowy places of the kingdom, and through the dusty layers of his memory, for a woman who might suit his own exceptional tastes; and wherever he looked, his thoughts came back to Nimue, the Lady of the Lake. He hurried into the forest, and called her from the shimmering waters.

"Nimue," he whispered, "I love you."

At first, the beautiful Nimue only laughed and teased him. But Merlin made a spell to bind her to his side with invisible bonds.

Then she grew frightened.

She knew that his powers of wizardry embraced darkness as well as light, and that his will was strong as mountains.

So she pretended that, in time, she might learn to return his love.

Meanwhile, she begged

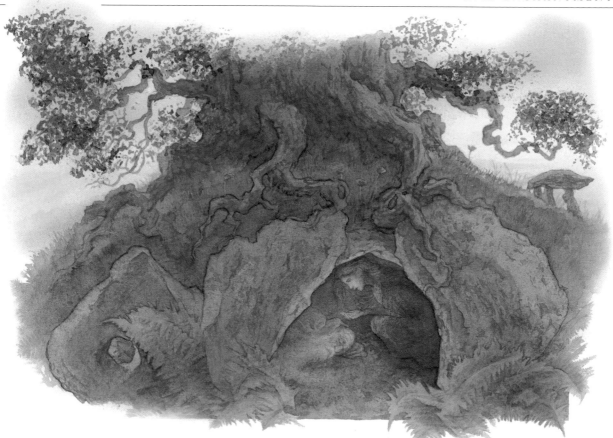

him to teach her the secrets of his magic. The besotted Merlin agreed.

He led the Lady through the countryside to Cornwall, and then to a secluded cave, sheltered by scented ferns. Deep inside, the rocks were lit by threads of silver, and cushioned with moss.

Here Nimue saw her chance.

She persuaded him to take her inside. Then she began to sing a song of enchantment that he himself had taught her, until she had lulled him into a deep, unnatural sleep. Creeping out, she worked other charms, until she had closed the cave mouth to a narrow, impenetrable crack.

In this way, the Lady of the Lake escaped Merlin's twisted love, and the wizard was condemned to sleep in troubled darkness forever.

At first, Arthur scarcely missed him. But as rumors spread of Merlin's end, he fell into a deep gloom.

His dismay did not go unnoticed. For within the inner circle of his court there lurked a handful of rogues who longed for a chance to dethrone him. They took the disappearance of Merlin as a sign that the time was now ripe to begin plotting against their king.

Nimue began to sing Merlin a song of enchantment.

Merlin's cave
One popular site for the cave where Nimue imprisons Merlin is "Merlin's Cave" at Tintagel, Cornwall. Merlin's disappearance signals the beginning of the end for the Round Table fellowship.

Morgan le Fay made a pact with the Devil.

Morgan le Fay

Morgan le Fay is Arthur's half-sister. They share the same mother, Igraine. Morgan's father was Igraine's first husband, Gorlois, Duke of Tintagel. In the earliest tales of Arthur, Morgan uses her knowledge of herbal medicine to cure wounded warriors. Later storytellers, however, made her a witch, insanely jealous of her half-brother's fame and success.

The most dangerous of these enemies was no stranger to King Arthur. Her name was Morgan le Fay and, shame to say, she was the king's own sister.

Morgan's heart was scarred with bitterness and envy: she ached to shatter Arthur's power and crumble his glory into dust. So she made a pact with the Devil, and studied the sinister skills of a witch.

She followed Arthur when he went hunting, changed herself into a deer, and lured him to chase after her into the deepest reaches of the forest, on and on, until he was dull-headed with tiredness. Then, on the bank of a rushing river – she vanished.

As he stood there, Arthur heard haunting strains of music: it came from a little ship that was sailing in to land. He stumbled toward it, as in a dream, and went aboard. There a woman, her face hidden by veils, fed him on honey-cakes, and sang him into a hazy sleep.

When he awoke, the ship and the veiled woman were no more. He found himself imprisoned in a gloomy dungeon, with his fairy sword Excalibur and its magic scabbard both gone!

*The veiled woman stood
there, a sword in her hand.*

Suddenly the dungeon door swung open. Arthur leapt to his feet. The veiled woman stood there, a sword in her hand.

"King Arthur," she mocked, "I suppose you want your beloved Excalibur back? Come then, take it – and fight your way to freedom!"

Arthur took the sword. Then he followed her up the dungeon steps into a castle courtyard. There a knight rushed at him with a fierce cry and they began to fight. At that moment, Arthur realized that the sword he had been given was a useless imitation – for the real Excalibur was gleaming in his opponent's hand!

Anger gave Arthur the strength of a lion. He hurled the false sword down, sprang at the knight, wrested the true Excalibur from his grip, and killed the stunned knight with a single blow.

The next moment, the woman scuttled forward with a shriek of laughter and threw off her veil. It was Morgan le Fay and she was clutching the magic scabbard! She ran – flew – with it, through the castle gate to the river. Arthur roared after her, but too late; she had already flung the scabbard into the swirling water.

Water witch
In Welsh tales Morgan appears as a dangerous lake fairy; French legends describe her as a mermaid who hugs fishermen to death; and mirages off the coast of Sicily have been blamed on "La Fata Morgana."

31

*There was a white
flash — and the cloak
burst into flames!*

Arthur gazed at the water where his
scabbard had disappeared. His wounds
throbbed, but he knew that he would suffer
far worse ones in the future without
Excalibur's scabbard to protect him. The Lady
of the Lake's warning echoed in his head and he
shivered.

But there was no place in his heart for fear. He
turned, strode back to Morgan le Fay's deserted
castle and mounted the dead knight's horse. Then,
using the sun to find his direction, he rode home to
Camelot.

There was no sign now of Morgan le Fay. But he could
sense her presence in the looming boulders he passed
along the way and in the weird hissing of the wind
through the trees.

As the evening shadows lengthened, he rode at last
into the warmth and light of Camelot. There he told his
sad tale and received Guinevere's comfort and his
good knights' advice. And so the night passed.

The next morning, a lady came to court
asking for the king. She was shown
into the great hall, where Arthur
and Guinevere were talking
with their knights.

The lady presented Arthur with a package, wrapped in silk and bound with satin cords.

"This gift is from my mistress, Morgan le Fay," she said. "She is sorry for the childish joke she played yesterday and hopes you will accept this present, your majesty, as her apology."

Arthur looked at the package with narrowed eyes. "Don't open it!" cried Guinevere. "Let this lady show us herself what is inside."

Without a word, Arthur handed it back. The lady threw Guinevere an angry glance as she carefully pulled apart the cords and binding. Inside was a magnificent cloak, lined with snow-white ermine and set with countless precious stones. Everyone gasped at its beauty.

The lady said, "Your majesty, may I demonstrate its true splendor by draping it over your noble shoulders?"

"No!" cried Guinevere at once. "How can we trust any messenger from that treacherous witch? I command you: prove this garment is not bewitched by putting it on yourself!"

"But your majesty, this is a man's cloak and far too heavy …"

"Obey the queen," said Arthur quietly.

The lady lowered her eyes. Very slowly and reluctantly, she picked up the cloak and slipped it on.

No sooner had she fastened it at her neck, than the rich fabric began to smolder and smoke. There was a white flash – and the cloak burst into flames!

Within a few moments, nothing was left of Morgan le Fay's messenger but a heap of dead gray ash.

King in ermine robes

Morgan's mockery
Cloaks trimmed with ermine (the fur of the stoat) have traditionally been used to adorn royal robes. Morgan is playing a gruesome joke on Arthur by sending him a symbol of royalty that bursts into flames.

Arthur and Guinevere
This episode shows how much Arthur depends on Guinevere's love and support. While they are in harmony, the kingdom and the fellowship of the Round Table are secure.

The Queen's Champion
The name Lancelot probably has Welsh origins; however his character was mainly developed by French poets in early medieval times. Courteous, brave, Queen Guinevere's own champion, Lancelot (above, played by Humbert Balsan in Lancelot du Lac, *1974) became a hero for all times.*

Lancelot of the Lake
Lancelot was the son of King Ban of Benwick. After Ban died, his widow left the infant Lancelot by a lake. He was found by Nimue, the Lady of the Lake, who brought him up and took him to Arthur's court. Lancelot of the Lake became the Round Table's greatest warrior.

When Morgan le Fay heard how her attempt to murder King Arthur had failed, she slunk away to nurse her fury.

"So," she muttered, "the queen thinks she can outwit me, does she? Well then, I shall have to beat her down as well as Arthur!"

She disguised herself as a lady of the court and hurried away to Camelot. There she mingled easily with the other ladies, charming them into friendship and persuading them to share with her the most intimate details of royal gossip.

Before long, she had learned something very interesting. For although Arthur admired and respected all his knights, it seemed there was one he held in particularly high regard. This knight's name was Sir Lancelot. His fighting skills were outstanding; he was also so intelligent, amusing, and charming that Arthur treated him as his closest and most trusted friend.

He was the perfect bait.

Morgan le Fay sweetened her disguise to win a morsel of Lancelot's friendship for herself.

Then she began to tease and inflame him with slanderous rumors about the queen.

"They say," said she, "that Guinevere is often lonely and melancholy, for Arthur is so preoccupied with ruling the kingdom that he has scarcely any time for her. I have even heard it whispered …" (she lowered her voice) "… that she would welcome the company of her husband's favorite knight."

Sir Lancelot listened and said nothing. But from then on, he became more watchful of the queen. He saw, as she moved about the court, that though she was always generous with her smiles, her sea-washed eyes were often soft with some wistful sadness. He began to wonder if what Morgan had told him was true.

Soon the wondering became a longing. When he was not on his knightly duties, now he always sought out the queen's presence. He was rewarded at first with pleasant remarks; then with longer conversations. Finally, Guinevere began to confide in him, sharing her secret concerns about all kinds of courtly matters – though on the subject of Arthur she was always discreetly silent.

As they talked, Lancelot became more and more aware of her spirit and her haunting beauty. He understood well why King Arthur had chosen Guinevere to be his wife.

Morgan le Fay loitered at Camelot just long enough to be satisfied that the evil seed she had sown had taken root. Then she withdrew to the shady chambers of her own fortress. She knew she had only to wait patiently while Lancelot and Guinevere's romance developed and swept them all toward a ruinous end.

Lancelot became more and more aware of Guinevere's spirit and her haunting beauty.

The Lady of Shalott by J. W. Waterhouse

The Lady of Shalott
Many women fell in love with Lancelot, but he refused them all. Elaine of Astolat, also known as the Lady of Shalott, died of grief.

Guided by angels – *Sir Galahad* by Arthur Hughes

The perfect knight

Galahad was the son of Lancelot and Elaine of Carbonek. Lancelot once made love to her, tricked by magic into believing she was Guinevere. Galahad was sent to live in a nunnery and raised as a devout Christian. When Galahad arrives at Camelot, Lancelot is shocked to see his son, and also feels guilt for his past misdeeds.

Galahad's place

Since the founding of the Round Table, one seat had remained empty, the Siege Perilous, reserved for the purest knight. Anyone else who sat there would die. In this illustration by Walter Crane, Galahad approaches this seat (in the foreground), accompanied by Nascien.

Chapter five

THE HOLY GRAIL

A S THE DAYS PASSED, Sir Lancelot grew tense with the impatience of love. This mood spread to the other knights, who always followed his example. So the warm fellowship of the Round Table began to crack under the strain of quarrels and petty fights.

Arthur saw this and called all his knights to renew their brotherhood at a grand feast. As they gathered together and the merrymaking was about to begin, a servant came running in.

"Your majesty," he cried, "a great marvel has appeared outside!"

The king and all the knights rushed out, down the grassy bank to the river. In the middle of the water, they saw a large stone of red marble with a sword jutting from the top. Suddenly the stone broke free of the current and drifted to the bank. King Arthur waded into the river and hauled it ashore.

"Something is written on this sword," he cried. "It says:
'ONLY THE BEST KNIGHT IN THE WORLD
MAY PULL ME OUT.'
Lancelot – you shall do it!"

"But your majesty, I am not…"

"I command you!"

There was silence as Sir Lancelot bent over the stone of red marble, gripped the sword and pulled. It did not move. The silence deepened.

"Try again," ordered the king.

Just then an old hermit named Nascien came hurrying along the riverbank. Beside him walked a young stranger – a knight with an open, handsome face.

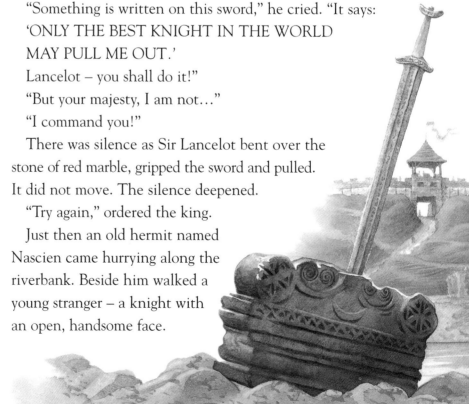

These two went straight to the marble stone. Lancelot turned pale as he stared at the young knight and stepped hastily out of his way. The young knight placed his foot upon the marble, and pulled on the sword. It came free at once.

"By Heaven!" cried King Arthur, "so you are the best knight in the world – and I do not even know your name!"

"You will find it within your own hall, sir," said the hermit, turning away.

King Arthur strode back to the castle, the young knight by his side. When they reached the Round Table, the knight did not hesitate but went straight to the Seat of Danger.

"Don't sit there unless you wish to die!" shouted many voices.

The young knight gazed around with his clear blue eyes. "But this place is reserved for me," he said.

Sure enough, the ominous inscription "SIEGE PERILOUS" had vanished. Instead, gold letters declared:
"THIS IS THE SEAT
OF SIR GALAHAD THE GOOD."

Beside the old hermit walked a young stranger.

The Grail vision
*The Quest of the Holy Grail
is the ultimate challenge for
any knight. Its appearance in
a vision witnessed by all at
Arthur's court urges the
knights to embark on the
final challenge – spiritual
perfection – instead of merely
settling for earthly glory.*

The Grail Castle
*The Holy Grail is kept in the
Castle of Carbonek, home of
King Pelles. Gawain cannot
say where the castle lies
because a spell of concealment
has been cast upon it by a
wizard named Tanaburs.
Only knights of great spiritual
worth are able to see the
castle.*

So good Sir Galahad took the seat that was rightfully his; then
the king and all the other knights were seated, too. As they waited
for the feast to be served, they all cast wondering glances at the
young knight, eager to test him with many questions.

But before any man could speak, there was a deafening clap of
thunder that shook the castle walls to their very core.

The echoes died and a stillness washed across the hall. From it
there grew a light, softly radiant as the morning sun.

Not one man spoke or moved.

The light burst open, spilled out – and became a vision.

It was like a promise, or a secret; a gift beyond understanding, borne
by angels, hidden under the white folds of a shimmering, silken cloth.
Every eye and every heart was drawn to it. Brighter and vaster it shone,
until its beauty was almost unbearable. Then slowly it faded, faded,
until nothing was left but deep silence and peace.

King Arthur whispered: "What have we seen? Who can explain it?"

At first, no one dared to answer. But then Sir Gawain, trembling,
stood up and said, "My lord, I believe we have seen a vision of the
Holy Grail. It is said that Jesus Christ drank from this golden
dish at the Last Supper, and that it holds some drops of his
sacred blood. I have heard that the Grail can work
miracles – and that just a sight of it can heal the
sick and bring perfect bliss to troubled minds."

"Where can the Grail be found?"
asked Arthur.

"It lies in a castle within a city,"
answered Gawain, "and the name of
both is Carbonek. No one knows
where this place is." He paused
and gazed around the table.
"But now I have seen a
glimpse of it, I swear I
cannot rest:

I must set out in search of it. My lord – I beg your permission and your blessing for a quest to find the Holy Grail!"

He had scarcely finished speaking before every knight was declaring, "I too, must join this quest!"

Arthur sat stroking his beard. Then he beat upon the Table for silence.

"If too many knights join this search," he said, "my kingdom will be badly weakened. Oh, what cruel fate has called you all away on the very day that Sir Galahad has arrived to complete our noble circle? And yet … surely this vision must come direct from God? If only the precious Grail could be found and brought here, I could use it to benefit all my people. Ah, then the glory of this realm would truly know no bounds!"

The light burst open, spilled out – and became a vision.

Joseph of Arimathea
Legend says that the Grail was brought to Britain by St. Joseph of Arimathea, a rich follower of Jesus. Years after Jesus' death, Joseph came to Britain, bringing the Grail and other holy relics, including a spear with which a Roman soldier named Longinus wounded Jesus on the Cross.

The Glastonbury Bowl, c. 250 BC

Treasure hunt
The word "grail" is from the Old French for "dish." The Grail Quest originates in Celtic myths telling of a hero's search for a magic bowl or cauldron that can supply unlimited food, heal wounds – even bring the dead to life. Bowls such as the bronze Glastonbury Bowl were used in pre-Christian worship.

Lancelot's confession
Lancelot sets off on the Grail Quest with high hopes, but little by little comes to realize that he is bound to fail because his love for Guinevere has marked him as a sinner. To improve his standing in the eyes of God, he visits Nascien the hermit (shown above), to whom he confesses all his sins. The hermit advises Lancelot to do penance by wearing a painful hair shirt, fasting, and praying.

Forbidden the Grail
Having made every effort to purge himself of sin, Lancelot finally finds the Castle of Carbonek and glimpses the Grail. However he ignores a heavenly warning not to go closer and is struck down, as shown in this painting. The anguished figure of Lancelot is on the left.

The next morning, all the Knights of the Round Table lined up below the walls of Camelot Castle. They came on horseback and dressed in full armor, like heroes riding to war. But this was a far nobler cause: to seek out one of the holiest relics of Christendom and bring it home to honor their kingdom.

Arthur's heart soared as he watched them ride away toward the rising sun. But when he turned to Guinevere, he saw that she was quietly weeping; and then he, too, was seized by sudden foreboding.

They were a long, long time on the Quest. Months passed. Then years passed.

At first there was no news at all of the knights. But other messages came to Arthur: of plots, of crimes and discontent in far-flung parts of the realm. He sent soldiers, but they did not carry the same authority as the Knights of the Round Table.

Then, one by one, the knights began to return.

They brought no prizes and no tales of glory. Instead they spoke of failure; of traveling endless miles without adventure, through barren wilderness and perilous forests without a glimpse of the Grail; they spoke of comrades who had met with miserable death.

One of the last to come home was Sir Lancelot.

He greeted King Arthur in a low, cracked voice and would not meet his eyes. Then he told a strange tale of dreams and visions; of how he had seen the Holy Grail and even come close to it – oh, so tantalizingly close! But before he could reach out and touch it, a bolt of lightning had struck him down – because, he said, of his sin.

Queen Guinevere knew all too well what this sin was and she turned away in shame.

King Arthur listened quietly. He said nothing. But thoughts ran like wildfire through his mind and his heart beat heavy with doom.

*One of the last
knights to come home
was Sir Lancelot.*

The Fisher King

The Guardian of the Grail is King Pelles, a descendant of Joseph of Arimathea. He is called the Fisher King because a previous guardian, Bron, once fed people with fish from the Grail. Some versions say that Pelles was wounded by a holy spear. At that moment the Grail vanished and the land around his castle was laid waste. Now he lies half dead. Only the knight who recovers the lost Grail can heal him.

Sir Bors's face was lined with the years, yet his face shone with a strange, calm light.

More months and years passed. The surviving knights went back to their work, doing many brave deeds to protect the people.

One day, when they were all gathered with Arthur and Guinevere at Camelot, there was a knocking at the door and in walked a knight whose face, framed by a white beard, they barely knew.

"My lord king!" said he. "My queen! Do you not remember me?"

King Arthur cried, "Sir Bors! We feared you were one of those who died on the Quest. A thousand welcomes to you!"

The good knight smiled. They saw that his face was lined with the years, yet his eyes shone with a strange, calm light.

"Forgive me for returning so late, my lord. I have been lost on a long and astonishing journey. I have struggled through wasteland, frozen wilderness, and burning deserts. I survived unspeakable horrors …

"But in time I met my brother knights, Sir Galahad and Sir Perceval, and went with them in a ship with sails of pure white silk, over endless misty seas. We came ashore at an unknown land and traveled through wild country, until we reached the fabled Castle of Carbonek. And there – at long, long last – we found the Holy Grail!"

A gasp ran around the Table.

Sir Bors went on, "My friends, this treasure is all we have imagined, and much, much

Detail from *Quest of the Holy Grail*, designed by Edward Burne-Jones.

The end of the quest

In Castle Carbonek, Galahad, Perceval, and Bors see angels bring the Grail down from heaven and place it on a table. Then Christ appears and feeds them from the Grail. Galahad then heals the Fisher King, using the Grail. Galahad is later taken up to heaven and Perceval and Bors enter a monastery. Perceval soon joins Galahad in heaven.

One knight was careful to hide his true thoughts – Sir Mordred.

"I sailed with Galahad and Perceval over endless misty seas."

more. To see it is to drink in the pure light of the sun, the sweet taste of newly gathered honey, the scent of every flower that ever bloomed since the Garden of Eden. It is perfect love, peace, harmony – perfect happiness!"

King Arthur cried, "Then bring it in at once, and show us!"

Sir Bors did not move. He said softly, "My lord Arthur, we three had no choice but to complete the Quest as God Himself willed it. So He led us on, carrying the Grail, to another distant realm. Here Sir Galahad was overwhelmed by its light and performed miracles too wonderful to speak of; after that, he passed away. I believe he is a saint in heaven now, with Sir Perceval beside him."

Arthur said, "Yes, yes, but where is the Grail now?"

"It is guarded by a saintly man who is called the Fisher King." Bors hesitated then went on: "He would not allow us to bring the treasure to you. He said – that Britain is not worthy of it. He said … that our beloved kingdom is too full of sinners."

"I see," said King Arthur. He gazed around the Table. Queen Guinevere had hidden her face in her hands. Most of the knights were shaking their heads in disbelief and sorrow.

But one knight was careful to hide his true thoughts. His name was Sir Mordred, and he burned with desire to seize King Arthur's crown.

In the murky recesses of his mind, Mordred laughed when he learned that Arthur's search for ultimate glory had failed. He could not wait to share this news with his accomplice, the evil Morgan le Fay.

Horn test
Morgan's drinking-horn challenge to the Round Table is typically cunning. Instead of testing the knights' well-known bravery and loyalty, she probes for weakness in an unexpected quarter – among the women of the court.

Celtic shield

Shield message
Shields were often embellished with designs to proclaim a knight's identity in battle. The image on Morgan's shield, however, depicts a conflict in love.

Drinking horn

Chapter six

THE END OF THE FELLOWSHIP

SIR MORDRED WROTE Morgan le Fay a letter:
"The king is weakened by despair. It is time to act!"
Morgan went to the chest where she kept her tools of sorcery and pulled out a drinking horn trimmed with gold. She wrapped it into a package, with a letter from herself, and sent it to the king.

Arthur was in council with his knights when a servant brought in the gift.

"This drinking horn is from my sister, Morgan le Fay," Arthur told them. "She writes that this is a magic horn that can test whether a lady is faithful to her husband. She advises me to compel our wives to drink from it, saying, 'any lady who spills the wine is proven to have a secret lover.' "

There was an uneasy silence.

Sir Lancelot stood up. "Sir, as you know I have no wife of my own, and so nothing to lose." He avoided the king's eyes as he spoke. "We all know that your sister is a devious witch. It would be a disgrace to let her blacken the ladies of Camelot with such a bogus test!"

"Those are shrewd words," said King Arthur, and he ordered his servant to throw the drinking horn onto the fire.

When she heard this, Morgan went to the mountain smiths, and ordered them to make her a shield, painted on the front with a knight stamping upon the heads of a king and a queen. She sent the shield as a second gift to Arthur.

Arthur gazed at it for a long time. Then he went among his men asking what this unsettling picture might mean.

Sir Mordred came sidling up. "Your majesty," he hissed. "It is quite plain that the king painted here represents yourself, and the queen is Lady Guinevere. As for the knight, he is one who holds you both in his power."

He paused, then went on crisply: "Everyone in Camelot – except for you, sir – realizes that the knight depicted here is your own favorite, Sir Lancelot. And that his power arises from his long, secret love affair with the queen."

A hush fell over the hall. Every man there turned to listen.

Arthur drew himself up. His voice was ominous. "You lie! Where is Sir Lancelot? I call on him to fight any man who accuses him of such treachery!"

"Oh," Sir Mordred said smoothly, "we all know that no one can defeat Lancelot in battle. But soon, your majesty, I will prove that what I say is true."

Single combat
Matters of honor between knights were often settled by single combat. It was held that the knight who was in the right would naturally win. In this story, Mordred is taking no chances and refuses to face the mighty Lancelot.

Morgan went to the mountain smiths, and ordered them to make her a shield.

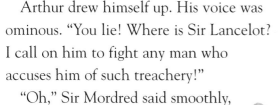

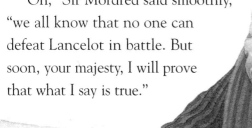

*Arthur returned home
in high spirits.*

A few days later, King Arthur
went hunting in a distant forest and
stayed away from Camelot overnight.
Guinevere did not go with him.

The king was joined by many friends, but Sir
Lancelot stayed behind. So did Sir Mordred and
twelve other false knights who shared his hatred of
the king.

Arthur returned home in high spirits. As he entered
the gates of Camelot he looked eagerly for Guinevere to
welcome him. But instead, Sir Mordred stepped out of the
shadows and cried, "My lord, I have dreadful news!"

The king did not flinch. He led Mordred to the Round
Table, summoning his other knights as witnesses.

"Speak," said Arthur coldly.

A holy Bible lay in the center of the table. Mordred laid his
hand upon it. "I swear," he said, "that everything I will tell you is
true. Last night, twelve comrades and myself went to spy upon
Sir Lancelot. We caught him red-handed: he was taking
advantage of your absence to meet secretly with your own
wedded wife, the queen!"

"Go on," said Arthur.

"I challenged Lancelot to come out and confess his guilt.
Instead, he devised a venomous trick – and by this he killed all
my comrades – murdered them, sir – twelve of your own good
knights, including Sir Agravain, your nephew!"

King Arthur passed a hand across his brow. He said, "I
am betrayed – by the two people I have loved most. By
Heaven, there was never a man so wretched as I am now! My
kingdom will be torn in two. And my marriage … But I must
decide, fast, what to do." His eyes swept around the Table.
"Who will advise me?"

Almost every eye was turned from him. But Mordred went on
eagerly, "The queen must be punished as well as Lancelot. She

willingly let him into her chamber. Her unfaithfulness is an act of treason against you!"

For a moment, Arthur seemed to sway. Then he took a deep breath and said, "It is clearly written in the Law books: the punishment for a woman's treason is execution, by burning at the stake.

"And when a knight turns against his own king, there is no question: the two must go to war. The deaths of my men must be avenged. I know that some of you sitting here will choose to side with Lancelot. You are all free to do what you will. As always, I welcome any knight who pledges loyalty to me."

He stood up, a towering, sun-touched figure. "I will do what I must." His voice quavered. "But the golden age is finished. And the fellowship of the Round Table is surely broken now forever."

Vengeful usurper
Merlin's prophecy that Mordred would one day threaten Arthur's throne now shows signs of coming true. One of Arthur's least noble acts was to cast the baby Mordred adrift on the sea in hopes that he might drown. Mordred miraculously survived. Regretting his cruelty, Arthur welcomed Mordred to his court, but Mordred has long desired revenge.

A dagger – symbol of deceit (Celtic, 1st century)

A "venomous trick"
When Mordred, Agravain, and eleven other knights surprise Lancelot and Guinevere in the queen's chamber, Lancelot has no armor, only a sword. He tricks one of the knights inside, kills him, takes his armor, then fights Mordred and his accomplices. Agravain, Arthur's nephew is among the slain.

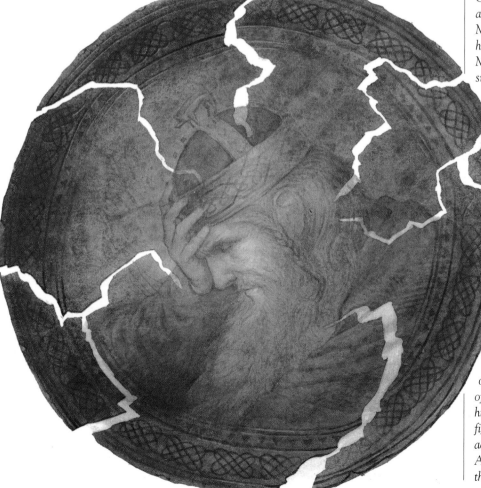

Lancelot to the rescue
Lancelot's love for Guinevere is too great for him to stand by while she is executed. He is a tragic figure, torn between love for the queen, loyalty to his friend and lord, Arthur, and love of God. This illustration by N. C. Wyeth shows him rescuing the queen.

The brothers' killer
Gaheris and Gareth were not only Gawain's brothers, and Lancelot's friends, but also Arthur's nephews. Their mother, Morgause, was Arthur's half-sister. When Lancelot killed Gawain's other brother, the scheming Agravain, Gawain forgave him, but he cannot forgive the deaths of Gaheris and Gareth.

The queen was imprisoned, and a date set for her execution. She cast away her jewels and her fine robes and sat straight-backed and barefoot like a hermit in her cell, speaking to no one.

As for King Arthur, the burning of his beloved queen was the most foul and pitiful task he had ever undertaken. His heart was broken beyond repair; he carried out his duties like a man of stone.

He went to Sir Gawain and said, "After Sir Lancelot, you were always my most loyal knight. I name you to take charge of the queen, and bring her to the stake for burning on the appointed day."

But Sir Gawain shook his head. "My lord, I cannot, for I love Queen Guinevere as if she were my own sister; and Sir Lancelot has always treated me with trust and honor. I beg you: follow Christ's teaching and forgive their sins; for no good will come from this punishment."

Arthur sighed. "On the day I became king, I swore an oath always faithfully to follow the Law. You must see, I would rather die than carry out this punishment, but for the sake of my kingdom, the Law compels me to do it."

Then he named Sir Mordred to be Guinevere's executioner instead, for no other knight would take it on.

The day of the burning dawned, with a lowering sky and a sharp wind. Hundreds of people gathered to watch. They saw Queen Guinevere led out to the stake in a snow-white smock. She held her head high, pale as a waning moon, with her long, burnished hair blowing in the wind.

And then they saw Sir Lancelot!

He came from nowhere, spurring his horse, his sword gleaming. A crowd of knights rushed forward, some to attack him, others in his defense. Lancelot hacked blindly at them all, foes and friends alike, for his only thought was to save the queen.

He killed many men. Among them were Sir Gawain's brothers, and Lancelot's own good friends, Sir Gaheris and Sir Gareth. As the terrified crowd fled, Lancelot slashed the ropes and freed Guinevere, threw a cloak around her shoulders, and swept her onto his horse. Then, with a cry of triumph, he went galloping away with her, through never-ending miles and hours, until they came to the stronghold of his castle, whose name was Joyous Garde.

Lancelot hacked blindly at foes and friends alike, for his only thought was to save the queen.

Joyous Garde

Lancelot carries Guinevere to his castle, Joyous Garde. According to legend, this was at Bamburgh on the coast of Northumberland. It was originally called "Dolorous (Sorrowful) Garde," until Lancelot captured it and freed it from an evil spell. The present castle (shown above) was built hundreds of years after Arthur's time, but the setting has changed little.

The purifying fire

At the time of this story – and for over 1,000 years afterward – burning at the stake was an accepted punishment. It was a penalty for treason and for serious crimes against the Christian religion, such as witchcraft. Christians believed the flames "purified" the victim of evil.

Last meeting
This 19th-century illustration
by Gustave Doré, shows
Guinevere begging Arthur's
forgiveness. Guinevere never
sees Arthur again, but
chooses to live in isolation
as a nun until she dies.

Women only
Since the 4th century,
some Christian
women have chosen
to live in nunneries
and devote their
lives to God as
nuns. A nunnery
also offered women
refuge; nunneries
were ruled by women
and men were excluded.

Now Britain was torn in two, for only half of
Arthur's knights stayed with him at Camelot. The rest
defected to Joyous Garde, where they pledged themselves
to become Lancelot's men and enemies of the king.

And so the long, happy peace was completely swept away,
as the knights on both sides prepared for war.

But before either side could lose or win, a messenger arrived
from the holy Pope in Rome. He commanded King Arthur and
Sir Lancelot to make peace, and ordered Lancelot to take
Queen Guinevere back to her husband. There were angry
mutterings within the ranks of both armies, but Arthur and
Lancelot were glad to obey.

The people lined the streets to cheer as Lancelot led Guinevere
home to the king. As her horse slowly climbed the hill, Arthur
walked down to meet her, holding out his hands. For a long moment
they looked deeply into each other's eyes.

Then Guinevere turned away.

She said, "Truly Arthur you have always been my only love.
I beg you to believe me!"

"I will take you back," said Arthur softly.

But Guinevere shook her head and sighed. "It is too late. I am
worn out by this game, wrenched in two by jealousy, tired of all men,
who look for any excuse to fight, and think they can squabble over a
lady like some lifeless toy! What happened to the code of honor and
respect you and all your knights once swore to follow?"

She pulled the wedding ring from her finger and let it drop to the
ground. "I am no longer your queen, nor any man's wife or lover. I
am going to join a house of holy nuns. From this day on, I give my
heart to no one, except for God."

It seemed as if the last vestiges of hope and joy were draining from
the king. Sir Lancelot went and knelt before him. "My lord," he
said. "From the depths of my heart, I am sorry!"

But the king's heart was empty. "Go!" he answered. "Leave
Britain forever, go over the sea. Leave me to

*Guinevere threw
down her
wedding ring.*

heal my poor, broken kingdom."

Lancelot bowed his head. "I will, sir."

"From this day on, I give my heart to no one, except for God."

He went quietly, shadowed by a sizable throng of men. After that, Arthur heard no more of him, except that he had sailed away, as ordered, to France.

There was peace for a while. But it could not last, for now Sir Gawain was twisted with grief. "My lord," he said, "you saw with your own eyes how Lancelot murdered my dear brothers when he snatched away the Queen. They had always supported him – yet he killed them in cold blood! Remember you are our uncle: it is your duty to assist me in taking revenge."

His complaint was echoed by Mordred – and also by many other knights, who feared their king was giving way to weakness. Arthur dwelt on the problem through many lonely nights. To save his honor, he found only one solution.

He called up a great army and led it to attack Lancelot in France.

Blood feud
Society in Arthur's time was held together by family relations supporting each other. As a result of Lancelot killing his nephews, Gaheris and Gareth, Arthur (portrayed above by Richard Harris in the movie Camelot) is caught up in a blood feud. Honor obliges him to make war on Lancelot.

When a king goes away to fight a war, he must leave behind a regent to take care of his realm. For this task, Arthur chose the man whose company he would most gladly be rid of for a while, that slanderous knight Sir Mordred.

As soon as Morgan le Fay heard that Mordred was effectively ruler of Britain, she hurried to him, offering to become his wife. But Mordred sent her packing, for he had no more need of her enchantments. Then Morgan flew into a seething fury and vowed that when she finally brought down King Arthur, she would destroy Mordred as well.

The months rolled by. Arthur failed to return. Mordred spread more malicious rumors until the whole of Britain was convinced that the war against Lancelot had failed – and that Arthur himself was dead.

Then Mordred had himself crowned king. He wallowed in his power, cruelly oppressing his own people. Soon, word of his actions reached France – where King Arthur was still very much alive.

The war had made no progress. Neither Arthur nor Lancelot could inspire his men to victory. Neither man had the heart to slaughter his one-time friend. Arthur longed for an excuse to return home.

So when a messenger hurried into his camp and gasped out the news that Mordred had usurped him, Arthur wasted no time.

Morgan vowed that when she brought down Arthur, she would destroy Mordred as well.

He ordered his men to turn around and march to the sea, then he set sail to rescue his kingdom.

Arthur and his weary soldiers sailed in to the coast of Britain – to find Mordred waiting with his own army to fight them off.

Morgan le Fay was there too, lurking, unseen, on the beach. She had made an enchantment to change her shape and hide herself among the cold, dark stones. There she waited for a chance to destroy both her brother and her former lover.

There was a short battle. Arthur's side quickly won. The good king did not wish to prolong the misery of war, so he offered Mordred a peace treaty, giving that villain a large area of rich land.

Then Arthur turned to address the two armies. "There can be no peace without trust," he told them. "This trust depends on all of you. So – I forbid any man to draw his sword until we have all left the battlefield. If this rule is broken by either side, then all trust will be broken, and we must return to the bitter slaughter of war."

"Agreed!" shouted all the men.

The peace treaty was signed. Great flagons of wine were brought, and handed around to seal it. Yet the celebration was tense.

As they drank, Morgan le Fay laughed in the caverns of her mind. Her moment had come!

She whispered a clutch of secret devil-words and changed her shape once again, from a stone into a snake, a poisonous adder. She crept up from the beach and slithered over the battlefield.

A soldier saw her. He jumped back, startled by her darting tongue, fearful of her deadly bite. Without stopping to think, he drew his sword and killed her.

Morgan died with a shriek of evil joy. For in her end lay the end of everything.

An adder

Symbol of evil
For her final act of wickedness, enchantress Morgan le Fay changes into the animal most closely linked with evil in Christian tradition – the snake.

Morgan changed her shape from a stone into a snake.

Final slaughter
In some versions of the legend, the final battle with Mordred is called the Battle of Camlann. No one knows for certain where Camlann might have been, but one possible site is Slaughter Bridge, over the River Camel in Cornwall. According to local lore, the blood of the slain stained the river red.

Excalibur's blade pierced the villain through the heart.

Chapter seven

THE LAST BATTLE

AS SOON AS THE SOLDIER drew his sword, the fragile peace treaty was broken. Then the full, terrible fury of battle broke out. The fighting lasted the whole day, with unspeakable agony and boundless death. It did not stop until thousands of men were dead – and only four were left alive.

These four were King Arthur, two of his knights, Sir Lucan and Sir Bedivere – and the wretched usurper, Mordred.

King Arthur stared grimly across the corpse-strewn field.

Mordred stalked toward him, dark against the darkness. Arthur gripped Excalibur. Its unearthly power surged through him. His muscles tautened with the memory of countless victories.

He strode forward to meet his final enemy. Excalibur flashed in the twilight, as Arthur thrust it under Mordred's shield – and pierced the villain through the heart.

But some Devil's mockery gave Mordred one last breath to fight back. He raised his own sword and brought it down, smashing Arthur's helmet to his head. Then Mordred died. And King Arthur fell to the ground in a mortal swoon.

Fight to the death
Mordred has an almost insane hatred for Arthur. In this Arthur Rackham illustration, he is impaled upon Arthur's spear, but finds the strength to deal him a mortal wound with his sword.

Birds of war
After battles, crows and ravens used to feed on the corpses. The raven in particular became linked with war. A Cornish tale relates that Arthur took the form of a raven after he was wounded.

*They came to a lake,
whose far shore was
shrouded in mist.*

Water spirits
*Bedivere throws Excalibur
into the lake – as depicted by
Arthur Wragg. Precious
objects were often cast into
lakes and rivers in Celtic
times as offerings to the gods.*

Chapter eight

THE ONCE AND FUTURE KING

I F ONLY KING ARTHUR had not lost his magic scabbard – for no
human skill could heal his wound. Sir Lucan and Sir Bedivere
knelt beside him. "Our king is dying," Lucan whispered.
Bedivere looked on in anguish.

"No," Arthur gasped, " I am not dying. Not yet. Never if … Take
me … to the Great Forest. Find … the Lady of the Lake." He was
too weak to tell them more. Lucan and Bedivere made a stretcher,
laid their king upon it, wrapped him in furs, and carried him away.

In time, they entered the calm, green shadows of the Great Forest.
On and on they trudged through dappled light, gnarled roots, and
ancient leaf-mold, ever deeper into the trees. At last they came to a
lake, whose far shore was shrouded in mist. Nearby stood a deserted
hermit's hut.

They took Arthur inside and laid him down to rest.

"Bedivere," rasped the king, "take my sword, Excalibur.

56

Throw it into the lake. Then come back and
tell me what you have seen."

Bedivere took Excalibur. Never in his life had he
held such an exquisite sword. He could not bear to throw
away such a treasure, so he hid it under a tree, then hurried
back to Arthur.

"Did you do it?" Arthur asked him.

"I did, sir."

"And what did you see?"

"Nothing but the waves and the wind, my lord."

"Then you have lied to me!" cried Arthur. "Do as I commanded."

Bedivere went back to the lake. Again he admired Excalibur's
unearthly beauty, again he hid it, again he lied to his king.

Arthur was growing weaker. "By Heaven," he gasped, "if you do
not obey, there will be no future …" He could speak no more.

Bedivere was moved by the mystery of his words. Without a
word he strode back to the lake shore. This time he took
Excalibur and threw it with all his strength, out into the
middle of the lake.

At once, a hand rose out of the swirling waters, caught
the sword, and brandished it three times. Then, out of
the mist, silken voices began to chant:

"Bring him for healing,
Over the water!"

Bedivere shivered.
He turned and ran back
to his wounded lord.

A hand rose out of the
swirling waters, caught
the sword, and brandished
it three times.

"Quick!" he called to Sir Lucan. "We must fetch the king!"

They carried Arthur down to the lake, stumbling in their eagerness. As they reached its edge, they saw a boat approaching, painted black as night. In it sat nine ladies, each one dressed in black robes and wearing the golden crown of a queen. Still they were chanting:

> *"Bring him for healing,*
> *Over the water!"*

"We are in time," sighed King Arthur.

The black boat rocked into the shore. Lucan and Bedivere carried King Arthur aboard, and laid him gently across the black queens' laps. "Away!" called the queen who sat at the helm. And the others sang in answer:

> *"Beyond all dreaming,*
> *The place of healing,*
> *Through the mist, to Avalon!"*

Then nine moon-white hands reached out and pushed away from the shore. They had no oars, no sail, no wind to blow them. Only some mysterious tide-force drew them away.

"Wait!" cried Sir Bedivere. "I beg you to tell us – will he die?"

The singing stopped. Silence fell like dew. The boat drifted on.

Suddenly, the queen who sat at the helm stood up and threw back her hood. It was the Lady of the Lake herself, Nimue. Her voice rang out:

"Arthur shall never die! Only let him sleep through the centuries in peace. And let all good people pray for his return. For he is The Once and Future King!"

AVALON! Who can say where it lies, that distant isle of fairy women and golden apples? Who can say how long Arthur lay there, while the queens of soothing night chanted over him and mixed their magic herbs, restoring the essence of his life? And afterward: where did they take him? Where is he resting now? Safe inside some hollow mountain, deep in the heart of his beloved kingdom, sleeping and always waiting.

For the time will come when the Great Forest will grow and spread across Britain once more, and Merlin will break free to bring good magic back to the world. Then King Arthur will wake and come forth to rule again, in all his former glory!

Suddenly, the queen who sat at the helm stood up and threw
back her hood. It was the Lady of the Lake herself, Nimue.

THE EVIDENCE FOR ARTHUR

When the Romans left Britain early in the 5th century, eastern Britain was invaded by Anglo-Saxon tribes. Their armies pushed westward, plundering and pillaging. A 6th-century writer named Gildas and a 9th-century monk named Nennius both mention a leader who halted the invaders, winning 12 battles. Gildas tells of a Roman Briton, Ambrosius Aurelianus, who saved the Britons. Nennius refers to "Artorius" (Latin for "Arthur") describing him, not as a king, but as a "dux bellorum" or "leader of battles."

Celtic warrior

Arthur the hero

Stories about a man capable of leading an effective resistance against the ruthless Anglo-Saxons spread rapidly. As time passed, Arthur was recalled in various ways – as a mythical hero, a battle leader, a king. Rooted in history, but essentially legendary, Arthur and his men became associated for-ever with courage, loyalty, strength, and justice.

IN SEARCH OF ARTHUR

The figure of King Arthur is shrouded in mystery. Despite years of research, it is still impossible to prove he ever existed. However, some historians believe he was a great warrior who lived in the late 5th century, and who led the Celtic Britons to victory in southwestern England against Anglo-Saxon invaders. Various places in Britain and France have been closely linked with Arthur's name, and with key events in his story.

Bosherton

Craig y Ddinas

Slaughter Bridge

Tintagel

Dozmary Pool

Loe Pool

Bosherton Lake

According to tradition, Sir Bedivere threw the sword Excalibur into this lily-covered lake as Arthur lay wounded. Other sites have been associated with this famous moment, such as Dozmary Pool and Loe Pool in Cornwall.

Slaughter Bridge

This site, on the River Camel, near the town of Camelford, Cornwall, is where Arthur may have fought the Battle of Camlann, his last battle against Mordred. A stone slab claims to mark Arthur's tomb.

The real Camelot

The site of Arthur's castle of Camelot may have been Cadbury in Dorset. Excavations show that the 5,000-year-old hill fort there was occupied during the 5th century, when a large hall with strong defenses was built. In the 14th century, Winchester Castle, Hampshire, became linked with Camelot, because it housed a fine round table. This table was built for King Edward III (1312-1377), who was inspired by Arthur's legend.

Gone but not forgotten – Guinevere and Arthur

Arthur's cave

Arthur and his knights are supposed to be concealed in several places around Britain, awaiting their glorious return. One tale tells that he and his men sleep in a cave in Craig y Ddinas, South Wales.

BRITAIN
(c. 5th century AD)

Arthur stemmed the Anglo-Saxon advance in western Britain.

Large eastern towns, such as Colchester, London, and Canterbury, fell to the Anglo-Saxons.

Colchester

Badbury Hill

Liddington Castle

London

Little Solsbury Hill

Glastonbury

Canterbury

Winchester

Cadbury

The Chalice Well
One story claims that Joseph of Arimathea hid the Holy Grail in this well near Glastonbury Tor.

The Holy Grail

FRANCE

Mont St. Michel

Arthur in battle

Mont St. Michel
This beautiful town in Normandy, France, is where Arthur is supposed to have slain a man-eating giant. Like the archangel Michael, after whom the place is named, Arthur came to represent good overcoming evil.

Glastonbury Abbey
Built, according to legend, on the site where Joseph of Arimathea established the first church in Britain, the Abbey was the scene of a national sensation in 1191 when the monks announced that they had found Arthur and Guinevere's tomb. A plaque marks the site to this day.

The ruins of Glastonbury Abbey

The Battle of Badon
Arthur's greatest victory against the Anglo-Saxons was the Battle of Badon. It probably took place around AD 499 and seems to have stemmed the westward advance of the Anglo-Saxons for 40 years. No one knows exactly where the battle was fought, though various places have been suggested, including Badbury Hill and Little Solsbury Hill.

Badbury Hill, Oxfordshire

The Isle of Avalon
After the last battle with Mordred, Arthur is taken to be healed on the Isle of Avalon. The legendary Isle was based on Glastonbury Tor in Somerset. In bygone times, the Tor was an island, surrounded by lakes and marshes. It was known as Inis Avalon, the apple-bearing island.

THE LEGEND OF ARTHUR

Arthur fights the Romans in Geoffrey's history.

In the 12th century, a Welsh monk named Geoffrey of Monmouth wrote *Historia Regum Britanniae*, The History of the Kings of Britain. From a few clues hidden in much older manuscripts, Geoffrey created a hero who conquered half of Europe! And so the legend of Arthur was born. Ever since, tales of King Arthur and his Knights of the Round Table have been told and retold, conjuring up visions of a golden age of chivalry. Painters, poets, composers, and moviemakers all over the world have been inspired by the legend's romance, magic, and excitement.

Lancelot the lover

When French poets, such as Chrétien de Troyes, rewrote the stories in the 12th and 13th centuries, they brought in a new character – Lancelot. As champion of Arthur's court, and secret lover of Queen Guinevere, he became more important than Arthur. Lancelot brought a new depth and tragedy to the heroic world of Camelot.

LE MORTE D'ARTHUR

The most famous version of King Arthur's legend is Le Morte d'Arthur, *written by Sir Thomas Malory in the mid-15th century. Malory (?-1470) seems to have been a shady character, often imprisoned for violent crimes. While in prison, he rewrote the legend and transformed all its many strands into a story about the downfall of a golden age.*

Sir Thomas Malory

Royal inspiration

Malory's work inspired monarchs all over Europe. Henry VII of England saw himself as Arthur reborn, reuniting the country after civil war. He even named his eldest son Arthur. His granddaughter, Elizabeth I claimed to be descended from Arthur himself.

King Henry VII (1457-1509)

Camelot, US

Modern rulers, too, have been identified with Arthur. In the early 1960s, US President John F. Kennedy's government was compared to the Round Table at Camelot. Many believed that his presidency heralded a new golden age of prosperity.

J. F. Kennedy (1917-63)

The Passing of Arthur *by Victorian artist James Archer*

Love and death

The legend of Arthur reached a peak of popularity in the 19th century. Victorian artists, such as the Pre-Raphaelites, and poets, such as Alfred Lord Tennyson, were especially drawn to the tragic side of the story. They created beautiful images of doomed love and glorious death.

One crazy knight

In classic European fiction, the character of Don Quixote tries to emulate the noble deeds of chivalrous knights like Arthur's – and just ends up looking ridiculous. He was created by Spanish novelist Cervantes (1547-1616) in 1605.

Don Quixote mounted on his anything-but-fiery steed, Rozinante.

On the stage

Arthurian stories have thrilled theater audiences – especially opera lovers, for whom German composer Richard Wagner (1813-83) created the masterpieces *Tristan and Isolde* (1859) and *Parsifal* (1882).

Actress Ellen Terry strikes a regal pose as Queen Guinevere in an 1895 play.

CinemaScope
M-G-M's FIRST MIGHTY PRODUCTION IN

Knights of the ROUND Table

ROBERT TAYLOR · AVA GARDNER · MEL FERRER
STANLEY BAKER · ANNE CRAWFORD

The Knights of the Round Table, starring Robert Taylor as Lancelot and Ava Gardner as Guinevere, promised epic romance and adventure.

Big-screen passion

Hollywood has celebrated the legend of King Arthur in all kinds of ways: *The Knights of the Round Table* (1953) was a glamorous epic, while *Camelot* (1967) turned Arthur, Guinevere, and Lancelot's tempestuous relationship into a big-budget musical.

CAMELOT.
RICHARD HARRIS · VANESSA REDGRAVE
FRANCO NERO · DAVID HEMMINGS
LIONEL JEFFRIES

A time-traveling dreamer (Bing Crosby) teaches Arthur's knights a thing or two in A Connecticut Yankee.

Fantasy and fun

Playful comedy characterized the 1949 musical *A Connecticut Yankee in King Arthur's Court*, from the fantasy novel by Mark Twain, while Walt Disney's *The Sword in the Stone* (1963) extracted maximum fun from the legend of the boy born to be king.

The Sword in the Stone
WALT DISNEY'S

© Walt Disney

Arthur borrows the sword in the churchyard for his brother, Kay, in The Sword in the Stone, based on T. H. White's novel.

1995's First Knight starred Sean Connery as Arthur and Richard Gere as Lancelot competing for the love of fair Guinevere (Julia Ormond).

Acknowledgments

Picture Credits

The publisher would like to thank the following for their kind permission to reproduce the photographs.

t = top, b = bottom, a = above, c = center, l = left, r = right.

Ancient Art & Architecture Collection: 15tr, 25br; R Sheridan 44cl; **Bodleian Library:** MS Douce 215 f.14 40tl; MS. Canon Lit 43 f.116 33cr; **Bridgeman Art Library:** Bibliothèque Nationale, Paris 24bl, 26tr, 27bl; Birmingham City Museums & Art Gallery 17tl, 26bl, 43tr; British Library, London 15cr, 62tl; John Duncan *Tristan and Isolde*, 1912 © The Estate of John Duncan. All Rights Reserved, DACS 1998 27tc; Fitzwilliam Museum, University of Cambridge 39tr; Lady Lever Art Gallery, Port Sunlight 16tl; Manchester City Art Galleries 62cr; Musée Condé, Chantilly 38tl, 45tr; Phillips, The International Fine Art Auctioneers 62cl (above); The Fine Art Society, London 33br; Walker Art Gallery, Liverpool 36tl; **British Library:** 42tl; **Camera Press:** 62bc; **CM Dixon:** 47cr; **English Heritage Photographic Library:** 12tl, 29br; **ET Archive:** Bibliothèque Nationale, Paris 26c; Tate Gallery 21br; **Mary Evans Picture Library:** 12cl, 27br, 36bl, 38bl, 48tl, 50cl (below), 50tl, 55tr, 56bl; Arthur Rackham Collection 31br; **Fortean Picture Library:** 16cl; Allen Kennedy 11br; Janet & Colin Bord 17c, 54tl, 60cl(below), 60bc, 61tr, 61br; **Germanisches National Museum Nürnberg:** 60tc; **Ronald Grant Archive:** 17bc, 27cl, 34tl; Columbia Pictures 63bl; MGM 63tr; Orion Pictures, 1980 22cl; Walt Disney 63br; Warner Bros 63cr (above); **Hever Castle Ltd:** 19tr; Images Colour Library: 7, 8cl, 16c, 22bl, 60c; **Katz Pictures:** Mansell Collection 26tl; **King Arthur's Great Halls, Tintagel:** 40bl; **Kobal Collection:** 1995 Columbia 18tl; Paramount, 1948 63 cr (below); Warner Bros. 51cr; **Mander & Mitchenson:** 26br, 63tl; Museum of London: 11tr, 27tl; **National Gallery, London:** 24tl; **National Museum of Copenhagen:** 44tl; **National Portrait Gallery, London:** 62cl(below); **National Trust Photographic Library:** David Noton 61cr; **Oxford Scientific Films:** G. Bernard 17tc(above), 53tr; Warren Faidley 17tr; **Photo RMN:** Hervè Lewandowski 60cl (above); **Pictor International:** 61bc; **Somerset County Museums Service:** 39cr; Tony Stone Images: 49tr; **Tate Gallery Publications:** WATERHOUSE, John William, The Lady of Shalott (1888) 35tr.

Jacket:

Ancient Art and Architecture: Front cl(above); R Sheridan Front tr; **ET Archive:** Bibliothèque Nationale, Paris Back cr (above); **Fortean Picture Library:** Back cr; **Museum of London:** Front tr (insert); **National Gallery, London:** Back br; **National Museum of Copenhagen:** Front tl.

Maps/additional illustrations: Sallie Alane Reason

Additional photography: Lisa Lanzarini 17br; Grock Lockhart/Rebecca Smith 21tr.

Dorling Kindersley would particularly like to thank the following people:

Tudor Humphries for artwork research; Fergus Day for editorial research; and Lyn Bresler for proof-reading.
Artist's models: Lizzy Bacon, John Brock, Mariel Chapman, Simm Peters, Lydia Walton, Theo Humphries.
Model: Susan Hoffmeister-Byrne